THREE OF THE BEST BRITS-V-JAPANESE COMMANDO COMIC BOOKS ADVENTURES

EDITED BY CALUM LAIRD, EDITOR OF COMMANDO

CARLTON
BOOKS

Published in 2011 by Carlton Books Limited
An imprint of the Carlton Publishing Group
20 Mortimer Street
London
W1T 3JW

COMMANDO is a trademark of and
© DC Thomson & Co. Ltd. 2011
Associated text, characters and artwork
© DC Thomson & Co. Ltd. 2011

A catalogue record for this book is available from the British Library.

ISBN: 978 1 84732 819 9

Printed and bound in the UK by CPI Mackays, Chatham ME5 8TD

Contents

Introduction

"Banzai!" — the traditional yell of Japanese fighting men intended to strike fear into the hearts of their enemies. And much used in Commando's legion of stories set in the steaming jungles of the Far East. The Banzai charge means only one thing — a ruthless, fanatical enemy is coming the way of a Commando hero in a merciless human wave.

However, that isn't all that you'll find in a Commando jungle tale. There will be men with secret fears and guilts, men who harbour grudges and contempt for their fellow soldiers. And yet, such is the way of Commando stories that, by the end of 63 pages, the fears will be overcome, the guilts wiped aside, the grudges settled and contempt turned to justified admiration.

Lieutenant Conrad Mellish, villain of the tale "Fight to the Finish" certainly has a grudge. One that looks as if it may cost his sergeant, Vic Barrett, his life. Mellish does everything to revenge himself on the luckless NCO, who puts up with everything thrown at him like a true Commando hero. Then, when Mellish is in the stickiest of situations, the only man who can help is the man he has done so much to alienate. Will he help?

For a secret guilt, look no further than "Where the Action is!" When a Commando officer lets some of his men, including his long-time sidekick, fall into the hands of the Japanese there's got to be a reckoning. But who can he blame but himself and his thirst for glory? Will Fate have something in store for Dave Fletcher, a chance to redeem himself? He'd better hope so.

"The Curse of Nanga-Jevi" might surprise you. The story has a helping of Banzai, a resentful Gurkha sergeant, a fanatical Japanese Colonel and a British lieutenant trying to save his command. There's also an ancient curse for good measure and, glory be, a Japanese officer who looks like he could be a hero.

Didn't see that coming? Well, get reading... "Banzai!"

Calum G Laird
Commando Editor

Commando WEAPONS FILE

SUB-MACHINE-GUNS OF WORLD WAR II

Calibre:	8mm
Capacity:	30 rounds
Length:	899mm
Weight:	4.18kg
Muzzle Velocity:	335 m per second
Rate of Fire:	450 r.p.m.

No. 12 — TYPE 100: The Japanese did not seem to realise the value of the sub-machine-gun until the later years of World War II. The Type 100 was named after the Japanese calendar year in which it was first produced (1940 by our calendar) and there were two versions of the gun. The first, shown here, was used by troops in S.E. Asia: the second, with a folding stock, was issued to the Jap paratroop units. Though the design was basic, and cheaply and simply made, it met limited success throughout its production. This represented the best attempt by the Japanese to produce a reliable sub-machine-gun, but it never reached European or American standards.

IT ALL BEGAN EARLIER IN THE WAR WHEN VIC BARRATT WAS A SECTION CORPORAL IN HIS REGIMENT'S FIRST BATTALION IN NORTH AFRICA.

THE FIGHTING IN THE DESERT WAS FLUID — THERE WAS NO CONTINUOUS FRONT. WITH UNITS SWANNING ALL OVER THE ARID WASTES, SMALL GROUPS HAD BECOME INVOLVED IN INDIVIDUAL ACTIONS.

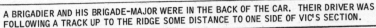

A BRIGADIER AND HIS BRIGADE-MAJOR WERE IN THE BACK OF THE CAR. THEIR DRIVER WAS FOLLOWING A TRACK UP TO THE RIDGE SOME DISTANCE TO ONE SIDE OF VIC'S SECTION.

WE'VE HAD NOTHING BUT CONFUSED REPORTS ALL MORNING, LANGDON. THE ONLY WAY I CAN SIZE UP THE SITUATION IS BY TAKING A LOOK FOR MYSELF.

ONLY WAY, SIR, AS YOU SAID.

NOBODY COULD HAVE CALLED BRIGADIER MELLISH A "BACK-AREA BRASS-HAT". HIS FAVOURITE SAYING WAS "WHEN IN DOUBT, GO AND FIND OUT."

VIC GAVE AN EXCLAMATION AS HE RECOGNISED THE CAR.

FOR CRYING OUT LOUD! THAT'S THE BRIG'S WAGON. THE JERRIES WILL SHOOT HOLES IN IT THE MINUTE THEY SEE IT.

HE ACTED ON THE SPUR OF THE MOMENT.

WHAT'S UP, CORP? YOU GONE BONKERS?

TO HIS RELIEF VIC SAW THE CAR SLACKEN SPEED – AND DIRECTLY AFTERWARDS A BURST OF FIRE BLASTED HIM OFF HIS FEET.

HE LAY FOR A FEW MINUTES WITH HIS EYES TIGHT-SHUT, THEN OPENED THEM TO FIND BRIGADIER MELLISH AT HIS SIDE.

HIS VOICE TRAILED OFF AND HE BLACKED OUT WITH THE PAIN OF HIS WOUNDS.

BACK IN ENGLAND, VIC MADE SLOW BUT STEADY PROGRESS IN THE MONTHS THAT FOLLOWED. THEN ONE MORNING...

I'VE NEWS FOR YOU, BARRATT. FIRSTLY, YOUR PROMOTION TO SERGEANT IS NOW OFFICIAL. SECONDLY, YOU'RE HAVING A VERY SPECIAL VISITOR THIS AFTERNOON. A BRIGADIER, NO LESS.

YOU MUST MEAN BRIGADIER MELLISH. HE USED TO COMMAND THE BRIGADE I WAS IN.

NEWLY BACK FROM NORTH AFRICA, MELLISH HAD LOST NO TIME IN ARRANGING TO LOOK UP THE YOUNG N.C.O. WHO HAD RISKED HIS LIFE FOR HIM.

HAVE THEY BEEN TAKING GOOD CARE OF YOU, BARRATT?

LIKE I WAS A V.I.P., SIR. THE DOCTORS RECKON I'LL BE FIGHTING FIT AGAIN INSIDE A MONTH.

THE DOCTORS WERE RIGHT, BUT WHEN VIC REPORTED FOR DUTY IT WAS TO THE REGIMENTAL DEPOT, NOT HIS BATTALION.

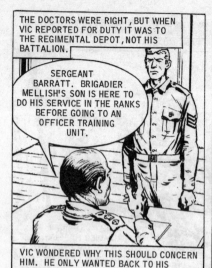

SERGEANT BARRATT. BRIGADIER MELLISH'S SON IS HERE TO DO HIS SERVICE IN THE RANKS BEFORE GOING TO AN OFFICER TRAINING UNIT.

VIC WONDERED WHY THIS SHOULD CONCERN HIM. HE ONLY WANTED BACK TO HIS BATTALION.

THE COMMANDER'S NEXT WORDS DASHED VIC'S HOPES OF A POSTING.

THE BRIGADIER HAS REQUESTED THAT YOU SHOULD BE APPOINTED TO HIS SON'S SQUAD AS AN INSTRUCTOR.

IT WAS A BIG COMPLIMENT TO VIC, BUT HE DIDN'T LOOK FORWARD TO BREAKING IN A BUNCH OF ROOKIES. HE'D HAVE LIKED IT EVEN LESS IF HE COULD HAVE FORESEEN THE OUTCOME.

THE FIRST TIME VIC CLAPPED EYES ON THE BRIGADIER'S SON HE WASN'T IMPRESSED — NOT ONE LITTLE BIT.

YOU, THERE! THIRD FROM THE LEFT IN THE FRONT RANK — PULL YOUR SHOULDERS BACK — HEAD UP — CHIN IN — THUMBS IN LINE WITH THE SEAM OF YOUR TROUSERS! WHAT'S YOUR NAME, LAD?

MELLISH.

UGH, WHAT A SPECIMEN, VIC THOUGHT. HIM AN OFFICER? HEAVEN FORBID.

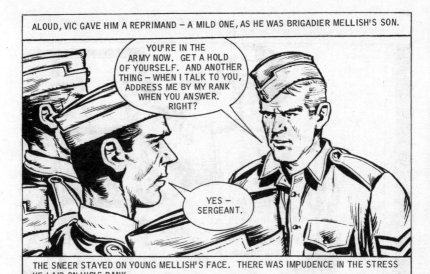

ALOUD, VIC GAVE HIM A REPRIMAND – A MILD ONE, AS HE WAS BRIGADIER MELLISH'S SON.

YOU'RE IN THE ARMY NOW. GET A HOLD OF YOURSELF. AND ANOTHER THING – WHEN I TALK TO YOU, ADDRESS ME BY MY RANK WHEN YOU ANSWER. RIGHT?

YES – SERGEANT.

THE SNEER STAYED ON YOUNG MELLISH'S FACE. THERE WAS IMPUDENCE IN THE STRESS HE LAID ON VIC'S RANK.

VIC BEGAN TO DRILL THE SQUAD, BUT BEFORE VERY LONG HE WAS INTERRUPTED BY A CLERK FROM THE ORDERLY ROOM.

GET THE STEP, AND SWING THOSE ARMS...

SERGEANT BARRATT, YOU'RE TO FALL OUT THE SQUAD. THERE'S A BRASS-HAT IN THE C.O.'s OFFICE ASKING TO SEE YOU.

THE BRASS-HAT WAS BRIGADIER MELLISH, AND IT SEEMED HE HAD BEEN WATCHING FROM THE DEPOT COMMANDER'S OFFICE WINDOW.

AH, SERGEANT, I WANTED A WORD WITH YOU. IT'S ABOUT MY SON. HE'S A SOFTIE. HIS MOTHER'S FAULT — HE'S BEEN A SPOILED BRAT ALL HIS LIFE. SO I'M RELYING ON YOU TO MAKE A MAN OF HIM, A REAL MAN.

THE BRIGADIER MADE IT ABUNDANTLY CLEAR THAT HIS SON WAS TO BE PUT THROUGH THE MILL.

NO SPECIAL PRIVILEGES FOR HIM. TEACH HIM DISCIPLINE THE HARD WAY — THAT'S AN ORDER. LIEUTENANT-COLONEL GUTHRIE HERE WILL BACK YOU TO THE LIMIT.

NEXT DAY VIC HAD TO TAKE THE SQUAD ON A ROUTE MARCH. HALFWAY THROUGH IT YOUNG MELLISH DROPPED OUT.

YOUNG MELLISH WAS STILL MISSING WHEN VIC LED THE SQUAD INTO THE DEPOT AND DISMISSED THEM.

VIC SPUN ROUND SMARTLY AS HE HEARD GUTHRIE'S CURT VOICE.

HE HAD TO FALL OUT, SIR. I'M GOING TO LEAVE WORD AT THE MAIN GATE THAT HE'S TO REPORT TO ME AS SOON AS HE ARRIVES...

HE'S HERE ALREADY. HE GOT A LIFT IN THAT RATION-TRUCK. GET HIM OUT HERE AND GIVE HIM AN HOUR'S DRILL — FULL EQUIPMENT, EVERY-THING AT THE DOUBLE.

LIEUTENANT-COLONEL GUTHRIE'S ORDERS WERE CARRIED OUT TO THE LETTER.

BREAK INTO DOUBLE-TIME — DOUBLE-MARCH!

YOUNG MELLISH WAS GIVEN A GRUELLING TIME, FOR VIC DIDN'T DARE SPARE HIM.

COME ON, GET THOSE KNEES UP. LEFT, RIGHT, LEFT, RIGHT! FASTER, MAN, FASTER!

MELLISH BEGAN TO POUR SWEAT, AND HE SEETHED INWARDLY WITH RAGE AS WELL.

HE BLAMED VIC AND VIC ALONE, UNAWARE THAT VIC WAS ONLY ACTING ON ORDERS.

GUTHRIE WAS WATCHING FROM HIS OFFICE WINDOW. THERE WERE OTHER SPECTATORS, AND THESE ADDED TO MELLISH'S FURY.

AT THE END OF THE HOUR, IT WAS A DROOPING, WILTING CONRAD MELLISH WHO FINALLY STAGGERED OFF THE PARADE GROUND.

HE'S JUST ABOUT AT HIS LAST GASP. SOME OF THESE SERGEANTS CAN BE TOO DARNED ROUGH ON A ROOKIE.

MELLISH WAS TOO EXHAUSTED TO HEAR THOSE WORDS OF SYMPATHY. THEY CAME FROM AN OLD SOLDIER NAMED CHALKY WHITE.

A GRIZZLED RESERVIST, CHALKY HAD BEEN RECALLED TO THE COLOURS IN 1939. MUCH TO HIS DISGUST HE'D BEEN STUCK IN THE BARRACKS EVER SINCE.

I'VE A GOOD MIND TO HAVE A WORD WITH THAT YOUNG SERGEANT.

YOU MAY BE AN OLD SOLDIER BUT YOU'RE STILL ONLY A PRIVATE, CHALKY. IT DON'T DO TO CROSS SWORDS WITH SERGEANTS.

BUT LIKE MANY AN OLD SOLDIER, CHALKY KNEW HOW TO BEND REGULATIONS, AND A FORTNIGHT LATER, AT THE BATTLE COURSE, HE SEIZED A CHANCE TO SPEAK HIS PIECE.

SARGE, I'VE BEEN WATCHING YOU HANDLING MELLISH — PICKIN' ON HIM, MAKIN' HIS LIFE A MISERY. NOW IT MAY BE NONE OF MY BUSINESS...

IT ISN'T. SO STICK TO SETTING UP THE TARGETS.

BUT CHALKY WENT ON DOGGEDLY.

SARGE, I'M ONLY TRYING TO PUT YOU WISE. MELLISH COULD MAKE TROUBLE...

LOOK — IT'S ON HIS OLD MAN'S ORDERS I'M PUTTING HIM THROUGH THE MILL. DO YOU THINK I ENJOY BEING SO HARD ON HIM?

VIC STOPPED HIMSELF, FEELING HE HAD LET HIS TONGUE RUN AWAY WITH HIM.

I'VE SHOT MY MOUTH OFF, SO FORGET WHAT I'VE SAID. I WOULDN'T WANT IT TO GET AROUND.

OK, SARGE. I'M SORRY I BROUGHT IT UP. I'LL KEEP QUIET.

THE NEW BATTLE COURSE WAS READY WITHIN A WEEK, AND VIC'S SQUAD WAS THE FIRST TO SAMPLE IT.

WE'RE DUE TO COME UNDER BREN FIRE AT ANY MINUTE. LIVE AMMO, AT THAT. BATTLE-INOCULATION, THE COLONEL CALLED IT. HOPE HE KNOWS WHAT HE'S DOING.

I HOPE THAT RAT BARRATT DOES. HE'S ON THE BREN.

AT THAT MOMENT VIC OPENED FIRE FROM THE SIDE.

THAT'S THE TICKET, SERGEANT. THERE'S ONE MAN LAGGING BEHIND THE OTHERS, THOUGH. IT'S...YES, IT'S YOUNG MELLISH. PUT A BURST BEHIND HIS HEELS AND SPEED HIM UP A BIT.

MELLISH GLANCED UNEASILY OVER HIS SHOULDER AS BULLETS HIT THE DIRT A COUPLE OF PACES BEHIND HIM.

I KNOW BARRATT'S GAME. HE TRYING TO SCARE ME.

AND TWO HUNDRED YARDS AWAY VIC WAS HAVING TO DO JUST WHAT GUTHRIE TOLD HIM, BUT MELLISH DIDN'T KNOW THIS.

COME ON, LET'S SEE HOW CLOSE YOU CAN REALLY GET.

RELUCTANTLY VIC OBEYED — AND THE EFFECT WAS IMMEDIATE.

FOR CRYING OUT LOUD!

MELLISH WAS SUDDENLY OUT IN FRONT, A FLYING FIGURE WHO COULD TAKE ANY OBSTACLE IN HIS STRIDE.

LAH-DI-DAH'S GOT ANTS IN HIS PANTS. LOOK AT HIM GO!

THE END OF THE COURSE WAS MARKED BY THE TARGETS CHALKY HAD SET UP, AND EVERY MAN HAD TO FIRE FIVE ROUNDS RAPID AT ONE OF THEM.

YOU DON'T HALF LOOK VICIOUS, MATE. ANYBODY WOULD THINK IT WAS A REAL JERRY YOU'D GOT IN YOUR SIGHTS, NOT A TARGET.

NOT A JERRY — BARRATT!

IN THE ENSUING WEEKS MELLISH'S BOTTLED-UP HATE GREW EVEN MORE INTENSE. THEN, HIS INITIAL TRAINING IN THE RANKS AT AN END, HE WAS INTERVIEWED BY GUTHRIE.

WELL, MY BOY, YOU'RE OFF TO O.C.T.U. TOMORROW AND I'M CONFIDENT YOU'LL DO WELL. YOU'RE TWICE THE MAN YOU WERE THREE MONTHS AGO. I HOPE YOU REALISE HOW MUCH YOU OWE TO SERGEANT BARRATT.

BUT IF GUTHRIE IMAGINED CONRAD MELLISH WAS GRATEFUL TO VIC HE COULDN'T HAVE BEEN MORE WRONG.

THE FOLLOWING MORNING MELLISH LEFT THE DEPOT WITH OTHER OFFICER-CANDIDATES.

THAT RAT BARRATT DOESN'T KNOW WHAT HE'S IN FOR. AS SOON AS I'M COMMISSIONED I'LL PULL ALL THE STRINGS I CAN, JUST TO GET HIM UNDER MY COMMAND. AND THEN I'LL MAKE HIM SQUIRM!

BUT BY THE TIME MELLISH WAS COMMISSIONED VIC WAS THOUSANDS OF MILES AWAY IN BURMA. IT WAS A FAR CRY FROM THE UNCHANGING ROUTINE OF THE DEPOT.

SERGEANT BARRATT, WE'RE DESPERATELY SHORT OF OFFICERS. YOU'RE FAIRLY NEW HERE, BUT I WANT YOU TO REPORT TO 'B' COMPANY FOR DUTY AS AN ACTING PLATOON COMMANDER. D'YOU THINK YOU'RE UP TO IT?

I'LL DO MY BEST, SIR.

BORED BY DEPOT ROUTINE, VIC HAD BEGGED FOR A POSTING OVERSEAS AND HAD BEEN DRAFTED TO THE REGIMENT'S FOURTH BATTALION. SO HAD CHALKY WHITE.

YOU MUST HAVE BEEN BONKERS, MATE, PESTERING TO GET SENT OUT HERE TO FLAMIN' BURMA.

BURMA...ITALY...I DIDN'T CARE WHERE IT WAS, AS LONG AS THERE WAS A BIT OF ACTION. SERGEANT BARRATT FELT THE SAME WAY. YOU'D HAVE GOT FED UP IN BARRACKS, TOO, SMITH, BELIEVE ME.

A BANNER-WAVING JAP LEAPT INTO THE ATTACK, HIS WAR-CRY ON HIS LIPS. IT WAS THE LAST SOUND HE EVER UTTERED.

CHALKY WAS SEEMINGLY UNHURT AND WAS ABLE TO MAKE FOR THE JUNGLE WITH VIC'S HELP.

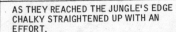

AS THEY REACHED THE JUNGLE'S EDGE CHALKY STRAIGHTENED UP WITH AN EFFORT.

I'M OK NOW, SARGE. GIMME MY BUNDOOK.

YOU CAN HAVE YOUR RIFLE, BUT YOU'RE NOT STAYING HERE. YOU'RE GOING BACK TO SEE THE DOC.

THE M.O. DIAGNOSED CONCUSSION AND A FORTNIGHT WENT BY BEFORE CHALKY RETURNED TO THE PLATOON.

GOOD TO SEE YOU AGAIN, CHALKY.

THANKS. HEY — YOUNG MELLISH IS HERE. HE SHOWED UP LAST NIGHT WITH THREE MORE NEW OFFICERS.

IT WAS ONLY TOO TRUE. AT THAT MOMENT SECOND LIEUTENANT CONRAD MELLISH WAS WITH THE COMMANDING OFFICER AND THE ADJUTANT AT BATTALION H.Q.

YOU CAN HAVE A PLATOON IN 'D' COMPANY...

EXCUSE ME, COLONEL, BUT MAY I MAKE A REQUEST? I UNDERSTAND YOU'VE A SERGEANT NAMED BARRATT IN 'B' COMPANY AND I'D LIKE TO HAVE HIM WITH ME.

AND SOON MELLISH MET HIS PLATOON SERGEANT.

WELL, WELL, SERGEANT BARRATT. LONG TIME NO SEE. I'M YOUR NEW PLATOON COMMANDER — ISN'T THAT NICE?

SURE, IT'LL BE NICE, AND I DON'T THINK.

THAT NIGHT CONRAD MELLISH HAD HIS FIRST TASTE OF LIFE IN THE FRONT LINE — AS SIX PLATOON'S NEW COMMANDER.

HELP ME... HELP ME... THIS IS JOHNNY... I'M BADLY WOUNDED... I CAN'T MOVE...

AN ENGLISH VOICE.

VIC SPOKE FROM A NEAR-BY SLIT WHICH HE WAS SHARING WITH CHALKY WHITE.

AND MELLISH CUT VIC SHORT WHEN HE TRIED TO EXPLAIN THAT NO ONE NAMED JOHNNY WAS MISSING.

TOO GOOD A SOLDIER TO DISOBEY AN ORDER, VIC MADE TO OBEY, CLOSELY FOLLOWED BY CHALKY.

BY MOONLIGHT THAT SHONE FITFULLY THROUGH BROKEN CLOUDS MELLISH WATCHED WITH A SARDONIC SMILE.

I DON'T MUCH CARE FOR THIS NEW OFFICER WE'VE BEEN LUMBERED WITH. HE SEEMS A RIGHT NASTY BIT O' WORK.

HAVING WANGLED A BURMA POSTING BY TRADING ON HIS FATHER'S NAME, MELLISH WAS OUT TO PAY OFF OLD SCORES NOW THAT VIC BARRATT WAS AT HIS MERCY.

VIC WAS TOO SMART TO HEAD STRAIGHT FOR THE VOICE. GRADUALLY HE AND CHALKY WORMED THEIR WAY INTO A POSITION BEHIND A MORTAR-BOMB CRATER.

HELP ME! WON'T SOMEBODY HELP? IT'S JOHNNY...

THE CRAFTY PERISHERS...

BACK IN THEIR OWN SLIT TRENCH, CHALKY LET OFF STEAM AGAIN — THOUGH IN AN UNDERTONE THIS TIME.

TRUST MELLISH TO TAKE THAT JAP OFFICER TO THE COMMAND POST HIMSELF. I'LL BET HE AIN'T GIVEN YOU ANY CREDIT FOR BRINGING HIM IN EITHER. AND I'LL TELL YOU SOMETHING ELSE, SARGE. MELLISH HAS GOT IT IN FOR YOU, SO WATCH HIM.

DAY BY DAY MELLISH'S SPITE REVEALED ITSELF IN MANY FORMS, AND WORD OF IT SOON BEGAN TO SPREAD, EVEN AMONG THE OFFICERS.

ACCORDING TO WHAT WE'VE JUST HEARD THERE'S A BIG BRITISH OFFENSIVE IN THE PIPELINE. WELL, IT'S HIGH TIME. THE JAPS HAVE HAD IT THEIR OWN WAY TOO LONG...

FORGET THE JAPS FOR A MOMENT, MELLISH. ROBBINS AND I WANT TO GIVE YOU A FRIENDLY TIP ABOUT YOUR HANDLING OF YOUR PLATOON, ESPECIALLY YOUR SERGEANT.

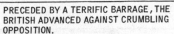

PRECEDED BY A TERRIFIC BARRAGE, THE BRITISH ADVANCED AGAINST CRUMBLING OPPOSITION.

BARRATT'S BEING USED AS A FLAMIN' MESSENGER-BOY. SOONER OR LATER HE'S BOUND TO BLOW HIS TOP.

AND GIVE MELLISH AN EXCUSE TO GET HIM BUSTED? NOT LIKELY!

STEADILY THE ADVANCE CONTINUED.

I SEE MISTER BLINKING MELLISH HAS DROPPED BACK A BIT. EITHER HE AIN'T GOT HIS SECOND WIND — OR ELSE HE'S JUST PLAIN WINDY ALTOGETHER.

IN THEIR PURSUIT OF A RETREATING FOE THE BRITISH PRESSED ON THROUGH A LAND OF WATERLOGGED RICE-FIELDS.

TYPICAL OF MELLISH — HE PUTS YOU IN CHARGE OF WINKLING OUT ANY JAP STRAGGLERS WHO MIGHT BE SKULKING AMONG THESE CROPS, BUT DOESN'T GET HIS OWN FEET WET. HE STICKS TO THE ROADS.

THAT MOUTH OF YOURS WILL GET YOU IN TROUBLE, CHALKY. EITHER KEEP YOUR VOICE DOWN, OR BETTER STILL, BELT UP.

AT LENGTH THEY CAME TO MORE JUNGLE. BY THEN CONTACT WITH THE ENEMY HAD BEEN LOST.

THERE WERE JAP SNIPERS ABOUT, SURE ENOUGH — SUICIDE TYPES, GLAD TO LAY DOWN THEIR LIVES TO DELAY THE BRITISH ADVANCE.

UNCHALLENGED, THE BULK OF THE PLATOON PASSED THE TREE THAT HELD THE JAP RIFLEMEN. THEN ALL AT ONCE CAME A VICIOUS BURST OF FIRE.

FOLIAGE HID THE MARKSMAN, BUT VIC THOUGHT HE SAW A SMOKE-WISP HOVER BRIEFLY BEFORE IT WAS BLOWN AWAY.

VIC THREW HIMSELF ON TO THE TRAIL AGAIN, WHERE THREE OF THE PLATOON LAY DEAD.

MEANWHILE, BACK ALONG THE TRAIL, MELLISH AND HIS PLATOON H.Q. HAD COME UNDER RIFLE FIRE.

TO GIVE MELLISH HIS DUE, HE SHOWED PRESENCE OF MIND AND INITIATIVE IN A DICEY SITUATION.

THE TREE BROKE, AND TWO SCREAMING FIGURES HURTLED TO THEIR DEATHS FROM ITS UPPER BRANCHES A HUNDRED FEET ABOVE THE GROUND.

THUS ENDED ONE OF MANY SAVAGE REARGUARD ACTIONS STAGED BY A CRAFTY FOE.

THE MONSOON RAINS WERE LASHING DOWN WHEN NEXT THE BRITISH SAW OPEN COUNTRY.

IT'S GREAT TO BE QUIT OF THIS STINKIN' JUNGLE, AND THIS TIME FOR KEEPS. THEY SAY WE'LL BE BACKED UP BY ARMOUR FROM HERE ON.

TANKS WOULD ONLY BOG DOWN IN THIS WEATHER. BESIDES, THEY'VE GOT TO BE BROUGHT FROM A LONG WAY BACK, AND WASHED-OUT ROADS AND TRAILS HAVE TO BE MADE GOOD FIRST.

IT WAS VIC'S GUESS THAT THE AUTHORITIES WOULD CALL A HALT UNTIL CONDITIONS IMPROVED.

VIC GUESSED RIGHT. THE ADVANCE WAS POSTPONED, AND ORDERS WERE GIVEN TO DIG IN.

THERE ARE SIGNS THE ENEMY MAY SOON MOUNT AN ATTACK.

MAJOR DUNN, 'B' COMPANY'S COMMANDER, HAD BEEN JOINED BY THE ADJUTANT, CAPTAIN RAMAGE.

SEE THAT RUINED TEMPLE? THE COLONEL'S WORRIED IN CASE THE JAPS USE IT AS AN OB-SERVATION POST TO CHECK ON OUR POSITIONS.

RAMAGE EXPLAINED THAT THE COLONEL WANTED A RECONNAISSANCE PATROL TO GO OUT AND CLEAR UP ANY JAPS WHO MIGHT STILL BE THERE.

...THEN YOU'RE TO ARRANGE FOR STANDING PATROLS TO TAKE TURNS THERE IN KEEPING TABS ON THE ENEMY.

FINE. I'LL SEE TO IT.

MELLISH WAS THE NEAREST PLATOON COMMANDER, AND, CALLING HIM OVER, MAJOR DUNN EXPLAINED THE SITUATION.

I GET THE IDEA, SIR. I'LL DETAIL BARRATT TO TAKE A SECTION OUT THERE STRAIGHT AWAY...

YOU'LL DO NOTHING OF THE SORT. YOU'LL TAKE A SECTION OUT THERE YOUR-SELF.

THE SPITEFUL MELLISH'S MOUTH FELL OPEN AS DUNN'S VOICE BECAME BITINGLY HARSH.

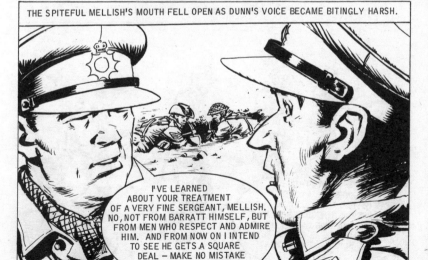

I'VE LEARNED ABOUT YOUR TREATMENT OF A VERY FINE SERGEANT, MELLISH. NO, NOT FROM BARRATT HIMSELF, BUT FROM MEN WHO RESPECT AND ADMIRE HIM. AND FROM NOW ON I INTEND TO SEE HE GETS A SQUARE DEAL — MAKE NO MISTAKE ABOUT THAT.

MELLISH FINALLY SET OUT ON HIS RECCE PATROL AFTER FURTHER STERN CRITICISM FROM HIS COMPANY COMMANDER.

I'LL BET HIS EARS AIN'T HALF BURNING AFTER THAT TELLING-OFF FROM THE MAJOR.

I DON'T THINK WE WERE MEANT TO HEAR, CHALKY, SO DON'T GO BLABBING ABOUT IT.

IT WAS TYPICAL OF VIC THAT HE DIDN'T GLOAT OVER MELLISH'S DISCOMFITURE.

THE RECONNAISSANCE PARTY SHOOK OUT INTO OPEN ORDER ON LEAVING THE THICKETS.

IT'S KNOWN THE JAP LINES ARE A LONG WAY BEYOND THAT HILLOCK, AND IT'S POSSIBLE THE RUINED TEMPLE'S DESERTED, BUT WE CAN'T TAKE IT FOR GRANTED. IF ANYONE SEES THE SLIGHTEST MOVEMENT, YELL.

MEANWHILE A CLAMMY MIST WAS GATHERING OVER THE LOWER GROUND BEHIND THEM.

THE RUINED TEMPLE WOULDN'T BE MUCH USE TO THE JAPS NOW. EVEN FROM HERE IT'S HARD TO SEE WHAT'S GOING ON BACK IN THE UNDERGROWTH.

IT'LL BE A DIFFERENT STORY WHEN THE MIST CLEARS. BUT NEVER MIND WHAT'S BEHIND US, CORPORAL JACKSON. WATCH FOR ANY SIGN OF LIFE UP AHEAD.

THERE WAS NO SIGN OF LIFE UNTIL THEY WERE A BARE FIFTY YARDS FROM THE RUIN. THEN THERE WAS SUDDEN LIFE – AND SUDDEN DEATH, AS A SHOWER OF BULLETS SPAT INTO THE PATROL.

KEEP GOING, THERE'S NO COVER HERE. BASH ON REGARDLESS.

ONCE AGAIN MELLISH WAS SHOWING PRESENCE OF MIND AND INITIATIVE.

AAAAH!

A JAP MACHINE GUN WAS CHOPPING DOWN HIS MEN RELENTLESSLY. MELLISH DROPPED HIS PISTOL AND GRABBED THE BREN.

I'LL BORROW THIS, GRAY. WE'LL BE BACK FOR YOU SOON.

THE ONLY TWO WHO WERE LEFT ON THEIR FEET WENT IN TOGETHER, MELLISH AND A BERSERK BARE-TOOTHED PRIVATE CALLED ROURKE — OR "FIGHTING MAN" TO HIS FRIENDS.

TAKE THAT, YE YELLOW DIVIL!

AAGH!

SHOT IN BOTH LEGS, MELLISH PASSED OUT. WHEN HE CAME ROUND HE HEARD ROURKE'S VOICE.

THEM TWO JAPS WERE THE ONLY ONES HERE. THERE'S A TANK ABOUT A MILE OFF. LOOKS LIKE IT MIGHT BE HEADED THIS WAY.

THERE WAS OUTRIGHT DISRESPECT IN ROURKE'S MANNER AS HE PICKED HIS WAY THROUGH THE RUINS AND SCRAMBLED PAST MELLISH.

WHERE ARE YOU GOING, ROURKE?

BACK TO REPORT.

MELLISH CALLED AFTER HIM FEEBLY.

YOU'RE... LEAVING ME HERE... KNOWING THE WAY THE JAPS TREAT THEIR PRISONERS?

ALL THE LADS IS DEAD EXCEPT LANCE-CORPORAL MURPHY. HE'S A GOOD MATE OF MINE, AND I CAN ONLY CARRY ONE MAN. AND DON'T TELL ME I'D GET A GONG FOR SAVIN' AN OFFICER — I'M NOT BOTHERED ABOUT MEDALS.

PAIN HAD DRAINED MELLISH'S FACE OF ITS COLOUR, YET FOR A MOMENT HE FLUSHED TO THE ROOTS OF HIS HAIR.

YOU'VE A PRETTY POOR OPINION OF ME, ROURKE, HAVEN'T YOU?

ME AND THE WHOLE PLATOON. WE ALL THINK TOO MUCH OF SERGEANT BARRATT TO GIVE A TINKER'S CUSS FOR YOU — SIR!

HOISTING MURPHY ON HIS SHOULDER, ROURKE CARRIED HIM DOWN TO THE PLATOON POSITION.

WHAT HAPPENED? WE HEARD SHOOTING, BUT COULDN'T SEE A THING FOR THIS MIST.

BEFORE ROURKE HAD FINISHED HIS REPORT VIC HAD PUSHED PAST HIM.

MELLISH IS UP THERE, STILL ALIVE?

YOU'RE NOT RISKING YOUR SKIN FOR HIM! ANYWAY THERE'S A JAP TANK THERE, SARGE. I SAW IT.

VIC STOPPED SHORT, AND DID SOME FAST THINKING. THEN HE RAPPED OUT ORDERS.

CHALKY, FETCH ME THAT NEW PIAT. FIGHTING MAN, TELL CORPORAL SOMERVILLE TO TAKE CHARGE HERE, AND GET MURPHY TO THE DOC. AND LET MAJOR DUNN KNOW.

OK, SERGEANT.

CHALKY RETURNED WITH THE P.I.A.T., OR PROJECTOR, INFANTRY, ANTI-TANK, AND ITS AMMO. HE GAVE VIC THE WEAPON BUT KEPT THE BOMB-CONTAINERS HIMSELF.

HAND OVER THE CARTONS. THIS IS A JOB I CAN TACKLE ALONE. IT WON'T TAKE TWO TO CARRY MELLISH. WHY SHOULD YOU WORRY ABOUT HIM, ANYHOW?

IF IT COMES TO THAT, WHY SHOULD YOU? I'M GOING WITH YOU, SARGE, AND THAT'S FLAT.

ARGUMENT WAS A WASTE OF TIME. THEY MADE FOR THE HILLOCK AT THE DOUBLE.

RECKON I KNOW WHY YOU'RE DOING THIS. IT'S BECAUSE YOU CAN'T HELP MAKING EX-CUSES FOR HIM ON ACCOUNT OF WHAT WENT ON AT THE DEPOT. THAT'S IT, AIN'T IT, SARGE?

PARTLY — AND THE RESPECT I'VE GOT FOR HIS FATHER. BUT CAN WE REACH THAT RUIN BEFORE THE TANK?

BUT LUCK WAS ON VIC'S SIDE. HALF A MILE AWAY THE JAP TANK WAS INEFFECTUALLY CHURNING MUD AND SLIME.

IT'S NO USE, DRIVER. THE TRACKS WON'T GRIP. BACK OFF AND LOOK FOR ANOTHER LINE OF APPROACH ON FIRMER GROUND.

YES, LIEUTENANT-SAN.

AND SO VIC AND CHALKY GAINED THE RUIN WITH TIME TO SPARE – BUT TIME FOR WHAT?

HE'S OUT COLD, CHALKY. YOU TAKE HIS ANKLES WHILE I...

HOLD IT, SARGE. I CAN HEAR AN ENGINE REVVING UP, BUT THE NOISE IS COMING FROM OVER THERE, NOT FROM THE JAP LINES.

VIC STUMBLED IN THE DIRECTION CHALKY HAD INDICATED, AND SAW THE OLD SWEAT HAD NOT BEEN MISTAKEN.

IN HIS QUEST FOR FIRM GROUND THE JAP TANK-DRIVER HAD BEEN FORCED TO WORK RIGHT ROUND THE HILLOCK – AND NOW HE WAS BETWEEN VIC AND THE BRITISH LINES.

MEANWHILE MELLISH HAD OPENED HIS EYES AGAIN.

MELLISH STARED INCREDULOUSLY.

BARRATT... CAME OUT FOR ME? I DON'T BELIEVE IT. HE NEVER HAD ANY USE FOR ME. HE MADE THAT PLAIN AT THE DEPOT...

YOU'RE DEAD WRONG. HE WAS ONLY CARRYING OUT YOUR FATHER'S ORDERS — HE DIDN'T WANT TO DO IT. MAYBE I SHOULDN'T BE TELLING YOU THIS, BUT PIN THE BLAME ON YOUR OLD MAN, NOT ON SERGEANT BARRATT.

WHEN VIC RETURNED, MELLISH KNEW EVERYTHING, BUT VIC WAS TOO KEYED-UP TO NOTICE ANY CHANGE IN HIS MANNER.

THE JAP TANK WILL BE ON TOP OF US ANY MINUTE.

THEN WE'D BEST PICK UP THE LIEUTENANT AND SCARPER.

VIC SHOOK HIS HEAD.

TOO LATE TO SCARPER, CHALKY. THE PIAT'S OUR ONLY ACE — IF WE GET A CHANCE TO PLAY IT.

THEY FLOPPED DOWN IN THE RUBBLE, AND THE P.I.A.T. WAS LOADED AS MELLISH PASSED OUT.

THE TANK DREW NEARER, NEARER, UNTIL JUST WITHIN RANGE. THAT WAS WHEN ITS HULL MACHINE GUN STUTTERED WICKEDLY. VIC HAD BEEN SEEN.

A BOMB FLASHED FROM THE P.I.A.T. A LAST-SECOND CHANGE OF COURSE BY THE
TANK-DRIVER PARTIALLY SPOILED VIC'S AIM BUT IT WAS A HIT ALL THE SAME.

WITH A SEVERED TRACK UNWRAPPING ITSELF, THE TANK SLEWED ROUND IN A SEMI-CIRCLE.

DEATH CAME IN A BLAST OF JAPANESE BULLETS...

...BUT THE BULLETS WERE FROM THE NAMBU MACHINE GUN IN MELLISH'S GRASP, AND THE ENEMY TANKMEN WERE ON THE RECEIVING END.

NOT LONG AFTERWARDS A PARTY SENT OUT BY MAJOR DUNN SHOWED UP, AND THANKS TO HIS FORESIGHT, IT INCLUDED A STRETCHER-TEAM.

NO, ATTEND TO SERGEANT BARRATT FIRST, THEN PRIVATE WHITE. THEY'RE WORSE OFF THAN I AM.

BUT MELLISH WAS WRONG. VIC AND CHALKY WERE BOTH BACK WITH THE BATTALION BEFORE HE HIMSELF WAS FIT AGAIN.

WELL, MELLISH, YOU'RE IN GOOD TIME FOR THE FINISH. THE JAPS ARE FAIRLY ON THE RUN. WE'RE STILL SHORT OF PLATOON COMMANDERS, THOUGH...

HOW ABOUT SIX PLATOON, SIR? I'D LIKE TO HAVE SERGEANT BARRATT UNDER MY COMMAND AGAIN.

SEEING THE MAJOR HESITATE, MELLISH WENT ON QUICKLY, EARNESTLY.

I WANT TO TRY AND MAKE IT UP TO HIM, SIR. I OWE HIM A LOT. I SAID THAT BEFORE TO COLONEL BRUCE, BUT THIS TIME I MEAN IT. GIVE ME A CHANCE TO PROVE IT, SIR.

AND PROVE IT HE DID. NO ONE COULD HAVE DOUBTED THAT, HAD THEY BEEN WITH SIX PLATOON ON THE DAY JAPAN SURRENDERED.

NO, I DO NOT GIVE UP SWORD TO COMMON SERGEANT. ONLY TO SOMEBODY WHO IS MY EQUAL IN RANK.

HERE WAS A HAUGHTY SUBALTERN OF THE BUSHIDO BREED, ONE OF MANY TAKEN PRISONER THAT DAY.

LISTEN, YOU ARROGANT LITTLE PIPSQUEAK. I OUTRANK MY SERGEANT, BUT I'D BE PROUD TO CALL MYSELF HIS EQUAL AS A MAN. NOW HAND OVER YOUR SWORD TO HIM, AND BE QUICK ABOUT IT, D'YOU HEAR?

JAPANESE SOLDIER

STEEL HELMET

HALF TENT

ENTRENCHING TOOL

FIELD SERVICE CAP

MESS TINS

AMMO POUCH

'TABI' JUNGLE BOOTS

'SENNINBARI' (BELT OF A THOUSAND STITCHES)

THIS heavily-laden figure is a Jap infantryman in full kit. He is armed with a Type 38 6.5 mm. rifle, used from the start of the war. Other interesting items include his half tent which could be pitched alone or joined with others, and it also doubled as a rain cape. His mess tin holds sufficient cooked rice for several days' rations, a valuable time-saver when on the march. Also shown are the extraordinary 'tabi' or jungle boots, in which the big toe is separated from the rest of the foot.

In the background is the "Senninbari," the embroidered belt of a thousand stitches, a form of good-luck charm which many soldiers wore round their waists in the belief that it made them safe from enemy bullets.

WHERE THE ACTION IS!

A SPRIG OF BRONZE OAK LEAVES ON A MAN'S MEDAL RIBBONS SHOW THAT HE HAS BEEN MENTIONED IN DESPATCHES FOR SPECIAL BRAVERY. DAVE FLETCHER'S FRIENDS KNEW THAT HIS NAME HAD BEEN MENTIONED THREE TIMES, IN THREE DIFFERENT CAMPAIGNS.

NOW HE WAS OUT FOR A FOURTH "MENTION" – BUT SOMETIMES A MAN CAN TRY JUST TOO HARD FOR ANOTHER BIT OF GLORY...

WHEN CAPTAIN DAVE FLETCHER'S COMMANDOS LANDED ON THE WEST COAST OF BURMA IN EARLY 1945, THEIR MISSION WAS TO CUT THE JAP LIFE-LINE OF REINFORCEMENTS.

HOLD IT! THERE'S THE ROAD ALL RIGHT. CHARLIE, GET THE SQUAD CRACKING.

RIGHT, SIR.

DAVE AND HIS SERGEANT, CHARLIE HIGGINS, HAD LED THE MEN THROUGH THE PADDY-FIELDS ALL NIGHT, AND NOW THEY HAD REACHED THE KANGAW ROAD.

THE COMMANDO EXPLOSIVES SQUAD WORKED FAST AND EFFICIENTLY WITH A SKILL BORN OF LONG EXPERIENCE. WHEN THE EXPECTED JAP COLUMN OF TROOP-LADEN TRUCKS ROLLED ALONG THE ROAD AN HOUR LATER, THEY GOT A NASTY SURPRISE.

AARGH!

UNABLE TO BRAKE IN TIME, THE SECOND TRUCK ROLLED INTO THE WRECK OF THE FIRST.

THE COMMANDO UNIT HAD DUG IN OVERLOOKING THE ROAD. NOW THEIR BULLETS AND GRENADES CAUSED HAVOC.

BUT THE FIGHT WASN'T OVER YET. LIEUTENANT MIZUNA, IN CHARGE OF THE LAST AND STILL INTACT TRUCK, HAD GOT ALL HIS MEN OUT SAFELY. HE WAS LASHING MORALE BACK INTO THEM WITH A BITTER TONGUE.

WE HAVE NOT YET LOST OUR HONOUR. THE PIGS ARE ON THE HILL-SIDE, WAITING FOR THE DEATH WE WILL BRING THEM!

RESOLUTELY THE JAP LIEUTENANT GATHERED IN GROUPS OF SURVIVORS FROM THE MANGLED TRUCKS AND FORMED THEM INTO A SINGLE FORCE AGAIN. THE JAPS BEGAN TO FIGHT BACK.

WELL, HOW ABOUT THAT! THESE BLOKES DON'T KNOW WHEN THEY'RE LICKED. I LIKE THAT.

THEY'RE EITHER TOO BRAVE OR TOO STUPID TO GIVE UP EASILY.

THE JAP STAFF CAR HALTED, THE MEN IN IT STANDING UP TO GAZE AHEAD, TAKING IN THE SITUATION.

IT'S A FULL-BLOWN GENERAL ALL RIGHT! TO CLOBBER HIM WOULD HAVE BEEN A REAL FEATHER IN OUR CAPS.

HE'LL PULL OUT AND SCARPER ALL THE WAY BACK HOME, I'LL BET.

A THREE-STAR GENERAL — DAVE'S EYES NARROWED. TO KILL OR CAPTURE HIM WOULD BE SOMETHING REALLY GLORIOUS.

THEY'RE TRYING TO TURN THE CAR ROUND AND PULL OUT. WE'D NEVER GET NEAR HIM.

MIGHT BE POSSIBLE, SIR, IF SOMEBODY NIPPED FAST ACROSS COUNTRY. THE ROAD TAKES A LONG LOOP ROUND A HILL UP AHEAD. WE MIGHT BE ABLE TO NAB HIM ON THE OTHER SIDE.

THE CAR SLEWED ACROSS THE ROAD, ITS OCCUPANTS ALREADY SPILLING OUT.

THE JAP OFFICERS DIVED FOR THE COVER OF THE UNDERGROWTH, ONLY THE DRIVER FAILING TO FIND SAFETY.

GENERAL YOSHIDA, HIS BREATH COMING PAINFULLY NOW, KNEW HE COULD GO ON NO FURTHER. HE YANKED THE PISTOL FROM HIS HOLSTER —

BY SHINTO, I WILL KILL THE WHITE PIG...

AS THE PISTOL CRACKED AND A BULLET WHISTLED DANGEROUSLY CLOSE TO HIS HEAD, DAVE SPRANG FOR THE SHELTER OF A TREE.

FRANTICALLY YOSHIDA PUMPED LEAD IN THE DIRECTION OF HIS TORMENTOR.

SO THE OLD DOG'S STILL GOT A BITE, EH?

YOU WILL NEVER TAKE KENJI YOSHIDA ALIVE!

THEN THERE WAS SILENCE.   THE JAP HAD EMPTIED HIS PISTOL USELESSLY.   APART FROM HIS SWORD, HE WAS NOW UNARMED, BUT STILL DEFIANT.

IF YOU UNDERSTAND ENGLISH, I WARN YOU TO SURRENDER.

NO, NEVER!

AS DAVE CAME FOR HIM, GENERAL YOSHIDA GRASPED THE HILT OF HIS SAMURAI SWORD – AND TURNED THE POINT INWARDS.

IF YOU RESIST, I FIRE!

I SPIT ON YOU, SON OF A DOG.

BUT DAVE WAS TOO LATE. GENERAL YOSHIDA HAD GONE TO HIS ANCESTORS, KILLED BY HIS OWN HAND.

I WANTED HIM ALIVE...

WHEN DAVE REJOINED THE OTHERS THEY RETRACED THEIR STEPS AS QUICKLY AS THEY COULD. CHARLIE HIGGINS WOULD BE HOLDING THE FORT.

WHAT HAPPENED, SIR? WHERE'S THE GENERAL?

HE'S DEAD. KILLED HIMSELF.

DAVE ANSWERED CURTLY. HE REALISED WHAT A WASTE OF TIME IT HAD BEEN TRYING TO CAPTURE THE JAP GENERAL.

WHEN THEY REACHED THE SPOT WHERE THEY LEFT CHARLIE AND THE OTHERS, WHAT THEY SAW STOPPED THEM IN THEIR TRACKS.

SUFFERING SNAKES, THEY'VE GOT THE SARGE AND MOST OF THE LADS! HOW THE DICKENS DID THAT HAPPEN?

DAVE SWALLOWED HARD — THEN ANSWERED SHORTY'S QUESTION.

BECAUSE OUR BLOKES WERE OUTNUMBERED. AND IT WAS MY FAULT! WE SHOULD HAVE PULLED OUT WHEN WE HAD THE CHANCE.

THEY TRIED TO INTERCEPT THE TRUCK WHERE THEY HAD AMBUSHED THE JAP GENERAL, BUT THE STRENGTH WAS NO LONGER IN THEM. IT HAD BEEN SAPPED BY A DAY AND NIGHT OF MARCHING AND HARD FIGHTING. THEY ARRIVED TOO LATE.

OH, NO! I'LL NEVER FORGIVE MYSELF.

TOO RIGHT. WHEN YOU WENT AFTER THAT GENERAL, YOU WENT AFTER A BLOOMING GONG AS WELL! YOU GOT THE JAP ALL RIGHT, BUT YOU'VE LOST US CHARLIE HIGGINS AND SOME MORE GOOD BLOKES — SIR!

IT WAS A BITTER TREK BACK TO BASE WHERE A TENSE DAVE FLETCHER REPORTED TO LIEUTENANT-COLONEL MIKE COLDRICK, HIS C.O.

ALL RIGHT, DAVE, TAKE A PEW AND STOP WORRYING. OK, YOU SUFFERED SOME LOSSES. BUT RESULTS JUSTIFIED IT.

AND THAT GENERAL WAS YOSHIDA, THEIR DIV. COMMANDER — A REAL CATCH! I GOT THE STORY FROM YOUR MEN, AND YOU'LL CERTAINLY GET A MENTION IN MY DESPATCH!

COLDRICK KNEW THE WHOLE STORY BY NOW, BUT HE DIDN'T KNOW DAVE...

THAT'S JUST THE POINT, SIR. I DON'T WANT A MENTION IN DESPATCHES. I COULDN'T ACCEPT IT!

FOR A MOMENT COLDRICK WAS STRUCK DUMB. BUT PUTTING DAVE'S OUTBURST DOWN TO BATTLE FATIGUE, HE SOON FOUND HIS VOICE AGAIN.

I KNOW YOU'VE GOT THREE MENTIONS ALREADY. ONE EACH FOR EUROPE, NORTH AFRICA AND ITALY. AND NOW ANOTHER FOR BURMA — FOUR MENTIONS! IT MIGHT BE A RECORD. YOU CAN'T TURN IT DOWN, DAVE...

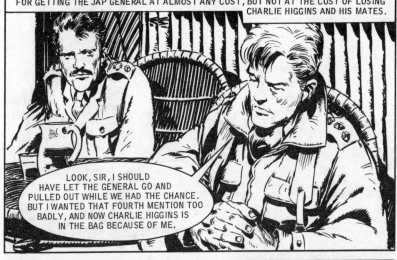

FOUR MENTIONS IN DESPATCHES! DAVE KNEW THAT HAD BEEN HIS AMBITION, HIS REASON FOR GETTING THE JAP GENERAL AT ALMOST ANY COST, BUT NOT AT THE COST OF LOSING CHARLIE HIGGINS AND HIS MATES.

LOOK, SIR, I SHOULD HAVE LET THE GENERAL GO AND PULLED OUT WHILE WE HAD THE CHANCE. BUT I WANTED THAT FOURTH MENTION TOO BADLY, AND NOW CHARLIE HIGGINS IS IN THE BAG BECAUSE OF ME.

COLDRICK LISTENED IN SILENCE AS DAVE WENT ON.

YOU WON'T KNOW THIS, BUT CHARLIE AND I JOINED THE RUTLANDS TOGETHER BEFORE THE COMMANDO LARK STARTED. HE WAS WITH ME EVERY TIME I GOT A MENTION. IN FRANCE, IN NINETEEN-FORTY, I WAS A CORPORAL AND HE WAS A PRIVATE...

CHARLIE'S HUNGER PANGS GOT THE BETTER OF HIM AND HE MADE TO GO AFTER THE SNIPER.

DON'T BE A CLOT! HE'LL SHOOT YOU BEFORE YOU GET TEN YARDS.

NOT IF I GET HIM FIRST. ANYWAY, IT'S BETTER THAN STARVING.

I KNOW WE NEED FOOD, AND I'LL BE THE ONE TO GET IT.

TELL YOU WHAT — I'LL TOSS YOU FOR IT. THAT'S FAIR.

IT CAME DOWN HEADS, AND CHARLIE HAD GUESSED RIGHT. WHILE THE OTHERS GAVE COVERING FIRE, HE SET OFF ON HIS MISSION.

GOT YOU THAT TIME, CORP. MY OLD DOUBLE-HEADED PENNY NEVER FAILS!

YOU...YOU TWISTER!

THEIR MISSION WAS TO RESCUE GENERAL BANNISTER, RECENTLY CAPTURED. INTELLIGENCE HAD SAID HE WAS BEING KEPT IN EL TEB FOR INTERROGATION.

THEY HIT THE NAZI STRONGHOLD LIKE A DEATH-DEALING WHIRLWIND, HEADING STRAIGHT DOWN THE STREET FOR THE BIG HOUSE.

HE DASHED INTO AN ALLEY AND THE CHILD RAN TO ITS MOTHER. THEN HE HEARD SOMEONE CALLING – IN ENGLISH.

CORPORAL, OVER HERE. I'M GENERAL BANNISTER!

EH?

GENERAL BANNISTER! DON'T WORRY, SIR. WE'LL HAVE YOU OUT OF THERE IN NO TIME.

CHARLIE RAN TO TELL THE OTHERS.

HEY, HE'S IN HERE! COME ON, THERE'S A WAY IN AT THE BACK.

AND THAT WAS THE STORY OF DAVE'S SECOND MENTION IN DESPATCHES.

...WE GOT BANNISTER OUT ALL RIGHT, THANKS TO CHARLIE HIGGINS AND HIS SOFT HEART. THAT'S HOW I GOT MY SECOND MENTION. BUT THE FOLLOWING YEAR IN ITALY, HE REALLY STUCK HIS NECK OUT...

THAT HAD BEEN IN 1944, AFTER THE LANDINGS AT ANZIO AND THE FALL OF ROME. DAVE AND HIS COMMANDOS HAD BEEN LANDED AFTER DARK ON THE WEST COAST OF ITALY. BY NOW, CHARLIE HIGGINS HAD THREE STRIPES.

IT'S ONE CHANCE IN A HUNDRED, BUT IT MIGHT COME OFF IF WE PLAY IT RIGHT. I'LL LOOK FOR A GOOD SPOT TO AMBUSH THE TRUCK WHILE YOU RECCE VEZIO AND SEE IF THE TRUCK'S STILL BACK THERE.

OK, SIR. I'LL HAVE A LOOK-SEE.

GERMAN SOLDIERS WERE BUSY SHUTTLING WOODEN CRATES INTO A BLACK VAN AND ANOTHER TRUCK.

CHARLIE HURRIED BACK UP THE ROAD AND REPORTED WHAT HE'D SEEN TO DAVE.

THE DOPE WE GOT IS CORRECT. THE VAN'S BEEN LAID UP TODAY BUT IT LOOKS AS IF THEY'RE GETTING READY TO MOVE ON AGAIN SOON.

WE'LL BE READY FOR 'EM, THEN.

TO AMBUSH A CONVOY AND ESCORT HIGHLY PRIZED BY THE NAZIS WOULD NOT BE EASY. EARLY NEXT MORNING DAVE MADE PLANS.

AS SOON AS THEY COME ROUND THE BEND, WE'LL ROLL THAT ROCK SLAP INTO THE CENTRE OF THE ROAD.

AND THE REST IS UP TO THESE PEASHOOTERS, EH?

CHARLIE TAPPED HIS TOMMY GUN SLYLY.

LATER THAT MORNING THE MAN SENT TO WATCH THE CONVOY LEAVE VEZIO REPORTED BACK AFTER A BREATHLESS SPRINT OVERLAND. CHARLIE LOOKED ON AS HE SPOKE TO DAVE.

THE VAN'S MOVED OUT, SIR, AND IT'S WELL-GUARDED. BUT THERE'S AN ITALIAN TRUCK TRAVELLING ABOUT HALF A MILE AHEAD OF THE REST OF THE CONVOY.

IT'S MAYBE JUST A GUINEA-PIG CHECKING FOR MINES. WE'LL LET THAT GO PAST BEFORE WE STRIKE.

LET IT GO, EH?

AS THEY WAITED FOR THE CONVOY, CHARLIE DECIDED TO HAVE A LOOK ROUND.

I'LL JUST RECCE ALONG HERE A BIT, DAVE. SEE EVERY-THING'S AS IT SHOULD BE.

ALL RIGHT, CHARLIE. BUT DON'T MISS THE PARTY.

THE MAN PLACED TO WATCH THE LONG HILL UP FROM VEZIO BLEW HIS WHISTLE.

THERE'S THE WARNING. NOW WHERE'S CHARLIE GOT TO? NOT LIKE HIM TO MISS THE FUN.

AS PREDICTED, THE COVERED ITALIAN TRUCK WAS LEADING, WELL AHEAD OF THE REST OF THE CONVOY.

THAT'S THE EYETIE CRATE. LET HIM PASS.

THE ITALIAN TRUCK ROLLED PAST. THEN CAME WHAT DAVE HAD BEEN WAITING FOR –

NOW, HEAVE!

CHARLIE REVEALED HIS SECRET.

LOOK, BOOZE! WHY DID YOU THINK I STOPPED THIS TRUCK?

YOU'RE IMPOSSIBLE!

THE TRUCK HAD A SPECIAL CARGO OF WINES FOR THE GERMAN TOP BRASS.

I SAW 'EM LOADING UP AT VEZIO. WE COULDN'T LET IT GO TO SAUSAGE-LAND, NOW COULD WE, SIR?

WITH THAT DAVE FINISHED THE STORY OF HIS THREE MENTIONS.

...SO NOW YOU KNOW ALL ABOUT ME AND CHARLIE HIGGINS. HE GOT HIS WINE, AND I GOT MY THIRD MENTION, WHICH I REALLY DIDN'T DESERVE.

DAVE GOT TO HIS FEET. HE HAD GOT A LOAD OFF HIS CHEST. BUT STILL CHARLIE WAS A
P.O.W. BECAUSE OF WHAT DAVE HAD DONE.

SO YOU SEE, SIR, WHY I DON'T WANT THIS FOURTH MENTION. IT JUST WOULDN'T BE RIGHT.

AS YOU PLEASE, DAVE...AND BY THE WAY, YOUR COMMANDOS AREN'T BEING BROUGHT UP TO STRENGTH AGAIN. WE'RE TO FIGHT AS ORDINARY INFANTRY FROM NOW ON.

NEXT MORNING HE PASSED ON THE NEWS TO THE REMNANTS OF HIS MEN. FOR THE FIRST
TIME IN HIS LIFE, DAVE SENSED THEIR RESENTMENT OF HIM.

SO THAT'S IT. WE JOIN UP WITH THE FOOTSLOGGERS FROM NOW ON.

JUST AS WELL, SIR. DON'T KNOW WHAT WE'D DO ON OUR USUAL STUNTS WITHOUT OLD CHARLIE HIGGINS.

DAVE KNEW EXACTLY WHAT SHORTY SCOTT HAD BEEN DRIVING AT, AND NOW HE WONDERED IF HE'D EVER HAVE WON A SINGLE MENTION IF CHARLIE HAD NOT BEEN THERE EACH TIME. AS HE CLIMBED ABOARD THE TRUCK TAKING HIS MEN UP TO THE FRONT NEXT DAY...

IF I COULD GET THE FOURTH MENTION WITHOUT CHARLIE'S HELP IT MIGHT PROVE SOMETHING...

BEG YOUR PARDON, SIR? WHAT DID YOU SAY?

HE HAD SPOKEN HIS THOUGHTS ALOUD. ANNOYED WITH HIMSELF, DAVE BRUSQUELY GAVE AN ORDER TO THE DRIVER.

OH, ER... NOTHING, NOTHING AT ALL. DRIVE ON AND GET INTO CONVOY WITH THE COLUMN.

YES, SIR.

IN THE NEXT FEW WEEKS, THE BRITISH ADVANCE SWEPT THE JAPS OUT OF ONE STRONGHOLD AFTER ANOTHER. DAVE'S COMMANDOS RODE THE TRUCKS BEHIND A SPEARHEAD OF TANKS.

HEY, SHORTY, I RECKON WE'VE DONE OK UP TO NOW WITHOUT CHARLIE HIGGINS. MISTER FLETCHER HASN'T PUT A FOOT WRONG.

HE HASN'T HAD A CHANCE YET. YOU WAIT FOR THE BIG PUSH, MATE.

THE BIG PUSH SHORTY HAD MENTIONED WAS AN ATTACK ON A MAIN JAP BASE AT KANYANG.

WE WILL STRIKE WITH THE ARMOURED BRIGADE LEADING. ONCE KANYANG FALLS, IT'LL BE THE START OF A MAJOR BREAK-THROUGH.

THE R.A.F. HELD THE WHIP-HAND IN THE AIR, BUT THE JAPS COULD STILL PUT AIRCRAFT UP, AS DAVE'S COLUMN FOUND OUT.

BUT IT WAS NEITHER BOMBS NOR BULLETS WHICH SPRAYED DOWN FROM THE SKY. THE ZEROES DROPPED NOTHING MORE HARMFUL THAN PIECES OF PAPER.

THEY WERE ALL ALIKE. ALL BORE THE SAME GRIM WARNING.

"BE WARNED. UNLESS THE ATTACK ON KANYANG IS CALLED OFF AND THE BRITISH WITHDRAW, ALL PRISONERS-OF-WAR HELD IN THE CAMP SOUTH OF KANYANG WILL BE EXECUTED IN REPRISAL!"

GOOD GRIEF!

BY JOVE, AND THEY'D DO IT, TOO...QUITE CAPABLE OF IT.

DAVE KNEW THAT. HE ALSO KNEW CHARLIE HIGGINS MUST BE IN THAT CAMP. BUT IT WAS COLDRICK'S DECISION —

NEVERTHELESS, THE RISK HAS GOT TO BE TAKEN. WE CAN'T CALL OFF THE ATTACK.

TEN MINUTES BEFORE MIDNIGHT, WHEN THE ONLY SOUNDS CAME FROM THE INSECTS IN THE UNDERGROWTH, DAVE'S COMMANDOS WENT INTO ACTION.

WE'VE GOT TO CLOBBER OUR WAY STRAIGHT THROUGH THE TOWN. THE CAMP IS THREE MILES ON THE FAR SIDE OF IT. SO WE CAN'T AFFORD ANY HOLD-UPS.

RIGHT. YOU CAN COUNT ON US, SIR.

WITH THE TANK'S GUNS BLAZING, THEY MADE THE BREAKOUT RIGHT ON MIDNIGHT. THE STARTLED JAPS NEVER KNEW WHAT HIT THEM.

AAARGH!

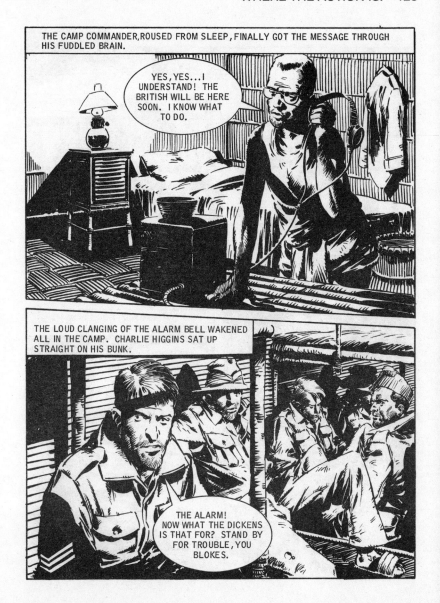

THE CAMP COMMANDER, ROUSED FROM SLEEP, FINALLY GOT THE MESSAGE THROUGH HIS FUDDLED BRAIN.

YES, YES... I UNDERSTAND! THE BRITISH WILL BE HERE SOON. I KNOW WHAT TO DO.

THE LOUD CLANGING OF THE ALARM BELL WAKENED ALL IN THE CAMP. CHARLIE HIGGINS SAT UP STRAIGHT ON HIS BUNK.

THE ALARM! NOW WHAT THE DICKENS IS THAT FOR? STAND BY FOR TROUBLE, YOU BLOKES.

QUICKLY THE COMMANDANT SET ABOUT ASSEMBLING THE PRISONERS.

THE JAP COMMANDER WAS DANCING WITH IMPATIENCE.

IN A SHAMBLING COLUMN, THE PRISONERS WERE HERDED THROUGH THE GATES.

I RECKON THEY'RE EXPECTING VISITORS! I'LL BET OUR BLOKES ARE ON THEIR WAY AND THEY'RE GETTING READY TO WELCOME 'EM.

ON THE FAR PERIMETER THEY WERE MARCHED INTO THE JUNGLE WHICH BACKED ON TO THE CAMP.

ANTI-TANK GUNS AND MACHINE GUNS? IT'S GOING TO BE DICEY FOR OUR LOT.

THE SPEARHEAD OF DAVE'S MEN HAD BROKEN THROUGH KANYANG AND WERE ON THE LAST VITAL STRETCH TO THE CAMP.

BUT THE MEN THEY WERE RACING TO SAVE HAD NOW BEEN TAKEN FURTHER INTO THE JUNGLE. AND CHARLIE HIGGINS, USUALLY SO CHEERFUL DESPITE ANY CIRCUMSTANCES, NOW HAD A GRIM LOOK ON HIS FACE AS THEY ENTERED A VILLAGE WHERE WORKING ELEPHANTS WERE QUARTERED.

AS THE MAN CHARLIE HAD WARNED YELLED AT THE TOP OF HIS VOICE, CHARLIE GRABBED AT THE UNCONSCIOUS JAP'S RIFLE.

THE JAPANESE RIFLE WAS STRANGE TO HIM, BUT CHARLIE HIGGINS WAS A MARKSMAN WITH EVERYTHING FROM A PEASHOOTER TO A SIX-POUNDER.

BEFORE THEY COULD EVEN BRING THEIR WEAPONS TO BEAR THE REMAINING TWO JAPS HAD GONE TO MEET THEIR ANCESTORS.

THAT'S THE WAY!

AARGH!

THEY NOW HAD FOUR RIFLES AND A CAMPFUL OF P.O.W.s, MANY OF THEM UNFIT FOR FIERCE FIGHTING.

I'LL TAKE A LOOK-SEE. YOU BLOKES TELL THE OTHERS TO TAKE COVER AND KEEP OUT OF THE WAY.

THE FIRING IN THE JUNGLE HAD BEEN DROWNED BY THE CHATTERING OF THE GUNS AS DAVE'S STRIKE-FORCE APPROACHED THE CAMP.

CHARLIE REACHED THE BACK FENCE IN TIME TO SEE THE FIRST ACT OF WHAT MIGHT TURN OUT TO BE A TRAGEDY.

THE TANK CREW BALED OUT UNDER FIRE AND RAN FOR THE COVER OF DAVE'S TROOP CARRIER.

MEANWHILE CHARLIE HAD RACED BACK ALONG THE TRACK.

THEN CHARLIE DISCLOSED HIS PLAN —

CARRYING THE BLANKETS, CHARLIE AND ALL THE FIT MEN MADE IT TO THE REAR OF THE CAMP.

HURRY UP! FILL THEM WITH THE DRIED GRASS AND BUNDLE THEM UP.

THE BUNDLES OF DRIED GRASS WERE SOON MADE UP AND SOME SPRINGY SAPLINGS BOWED OVER. THEN CHARLIE DEFTLY APPLIED A MATCH...

OK, FIREBALL ONE'S READY TO GO!

THE BURNING BUNDLE SOARED UP AND OVER, LANDING ON THE STRAW ROOF ON THE CENTRE HUT. AS THE ROOF TOOK FIRE, MORE "FIREBALLS" FOLLOWED.

OUTSIDE THE CAMP AN ASTONISHED DAVE FLETCHER WATCHED THE FIRES RAGING.

BADGE OF HONOUR

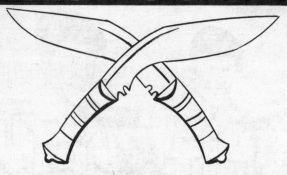

No. 2 — THE BRIGADE OF GURKHAS

"IT is better to die than live a coward"! This is the proud motto of the Gurkhas, the famous fighting men from Nepal who in their long history have never had a single case of cowardice, desertion or mutiny in their ranks. During the Second World War ten Gurkha soldiers won the Victoria Cross, the most coveted of all medals.

Their terrific reputation is partly based on the dreaded kukri, a boomerang-shaped knife whose sharp-edged blade can decapitate an enemy with one swift blow. Their badge shown above is made up of two crossed kukris — apt recognition of the awe with which friend and foe alike regard this fearsome weapon.

LIEUTENANT TOM SCOTT AND HIS GURKHA SERGEANT, GANJU THAPA, WERE PART OF A BRITISH FORCE, BLAZING THEIR WAY ACROSS BURMA IN AN ATTEMPT TO REACH THE JAP STRONGHOLD OF NANGA-JEVI.
LIEUTENANT OSAMU TAKITO AND HIS MEN WERE JUST AS DETERMINED TO STOP THEM. YET FATE HAD DECREED THAT THESE THREE MEN SHOULD FACE DEATH TOGETHER...ALL BECAUSE OF THE EMERALD-ENCRUSTED SNAKE OF NANGA-JEVI!

THE CURSE OF NANGA-JEVI

FEAR OF DISCOVERY WAS FORGOTTEN — THEY WORKED SILENTLY AND SWIFTLY UNTIL THE LAST EMERALD WAS RE-MOVED.

THAT'S THE LAST ONE.

GOOD! NOW LET'S GET AWAY FROM HERE BEFORE THE NEPALTA TRIBESMEN DISCOVER WHAT WE HAVE DONE TO THEIR GOD.

THE GURU OF NANGA-JEVI HAD NOT MOVED, BUT AS THE PLUNDERERS HURRIED AWAY, HE ROSE DRAMATICALLY TO HIS FEET.

NANGA-JEVI WILL NOT BE MOCKED!

AS THE GURU TURNED TO FACE THEM, THEY BECAME AWARE ONLY OF HIS EYES BURNING INTO THEIR VERY SOULS.

NANGA-JEVI CURSES THE HOUSE OF HARRINGTON AND THE HOUSE OF TAKITO. YOUR WICKEDNESS SHALL NOT GO UNPUNISHED.

ANGRY AND AFRAID, THE JAP MOVED TOWARDS THE OLD MAN AND SWUNG HIS RIFLE.

DOG, I WILL SILENCE YOUR TONGUE FOREVER!

TAKITO MOVED AS IF TO PUSH THE HOLY MAN OVER THE EDGE OF THE PRECIPICE BUT THEIR LITTLE GURKHA GUIDE GANJU GOT THERE FIRST.

YOU WILL NOT KILL THE HOLY MAN!

COME ON, TAKITO. LEAVE THE GURU BE. IF HE DIES WE'D NEVER GET OUT OF THIS REGION ALIVE...THE NEPALTA TRIBESMEN WOULD SEE TO THAT!

THE JAP, FRUSTRATED, TURNED HIS GUN ANGRILY ON GANJU, FORCING HIM TO MOVE AHEAD OF THEM.

AS DISTANCE GAVE THEM CONFIDENCE TAKITO OFFERED AN EXPLANATION, ALTHOUGH HIS OWN EASTERN BLOOD WARNED HIM THAT THE MYSTIC HAD POWERS BEYOND ORDINARY UNDERSTANDING.

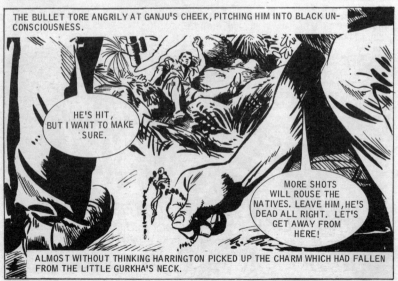

RETURNING TO THEIR CAMP, THEY PREPARED TO LEAVE, BUT THE OMINOUS SOUND OF DRUMS REACHED THEIR EARS FROM THE DEPTHS OF THE JUNGLE.

MONKEY ROCK, A MASSIVE ROCK FORMATION SHAPED VAGUELY LIKE A MONKEY, MADE A GOOD LANDMARK.

THEY WASTED NO TIME IN LEAVING NEPALTA, THOUGH BOTH WERE DETERMINED TO RETURN LATER. BUT IT SEEMED THE CURSE OF NANGA-JEVI DID FOLLOW THEM, BRINGING WITH IT SICKNESS AND MISFORTUNE, ALLOWING MONKEY ROCK TO KEEP ITS SECRET FOR OVER A DECADE.

GENERAL MARSDEN THEN INTRODUCED THE TOUGH, RUGGED LIEUTENANT-COLONEL RICHARDS.

A SPECIAL TASK FORCE WILL BE FORMED WITH EVERY MAN A TRAINED JUNGLE FIGHTER, CAPABLE OF PENETRATING DEEP INTO ENEMY TERRITORY...

SO SOLDIERS WERE BROUGHT TO BURMA FROM EVERY QUARTER, EACH ONE SPECIALLY CHOSEN, EACH ONE PROVEN IN BATTLE.

THIS IS AS FAR AS YOU GO, LADS. YOUR HOLIDAYS ARE OVER.

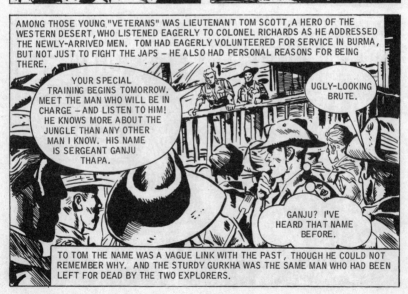

AMONG THOSE YOUNG "VETERANS" WAS LIEUTENANT TOM SCOTT, A HERO OF THE WESTERN DESERT, WHO LISTENED EAGERLY TO COLONEL RICHARDS AS HE ADDRESSED THE NEWLY-ARRIVED MEN. TOM HAD EAGERLY VOLUNTEERED FOR SERVICE IN BURMA, BUT NOT JUST TO FIGHT THE JAPS — HE ALSO HAD PERSONAL REASONS FOR BEING THERE.

YOUR SPECIAL TRAINING BEGINS TOMORROW. MEET THE MAN WHO WILL BE IN CHARGE — AND LISTEN TO HIM! HE KNOWS MORE ABOUT THE JUNGLE THAN ANY OTHER MAN I KNOW. HIS NAME IS SERGEANT GANJU THAPA.

UGLY-LOOKING BRUTE.

GANJU? I'VE HEARD THAT NAME BEFORE.

TO TOM THE NAME WAS A VAGUE LINK WITH THE PAST, THOUGH HE COULD NOT REMEMBER WHY. AND THE STURDY GURKHA WAS THE SAME MAN WHO HAD BEEN LEFT FOR DEAD BY THE TWO EXPLORERS.

MEN WHO HAD CONSIDERED THEMSELVES TOUGH AND FIT WERE MADE TO SWEAT AND ACHE AS THEY WERE TAUGHT THE SECRETS OF JUNGLE WARFARE.

COLONEL RICHARDS AND HIS SECOND-IN-COMMAND, MAJOR DAWSON, KEPT A KEEN EYE ON THE TRAINING.

AT LAST THEY WERE READY. MANY DROPPED OUT, UNABLE TO STAND THE PACE, BUT THE SURVIVORS WERE WELL-EQUIPPED TO TAKE ON THE MIGHT OF JAPAN.

WE'LL TRAVEL IN TWO SECTIONS BY TWO DIFFERENT ROUTES. MAJOR DAWSON WILL LEAD EAGLE SECTION AND I WILL COMMAND SNOWDROP. THE JUNGLE BETWEEN OUR-SELVES AND OUR TARGET IS INFESTED WITH JAPS, SO TRY TO AVOID THEM IF POSSIBLE. IF NOT, TAKE THE NECESSARY ACTION. ANY QUESTIONS?

WHERE ARE WE GOING, COLONEL?

THIS IS OUR TARGET. A MOUNTAIN CALLED NANGA-JEVI. IT IS A KEY POSITION COMMANDING TWO RIVERS AND THE ONLY ACCESSIBLE VALLEY. ONCE IT IS OURS, ONE OF THE MAIN JAP COMMUNICATION LINES WILL BE CUT.

THEIR TASK WOULD BE TO CAPTURE THE MOUNTAIN AND HOLD IT UNTIL THE MAIN BRITISH FORCE COULD MOVE FORWARD IN STRENGTH.

AND SO BEGAN ONE OF THE MOST DANGEROUS AND DIFFICULT MISSIONS OF THE WAR —

TOM SCOTT AND GANJU, BOTH OF EAGLE SECTION, SOON PROVED TO BE A FORMIDABLE TEAM.

TOM FOUGHT WITH NANGA-JEVI AS HIS GOAL AND NO JAPS WERE GOING TO STAND IN HIS WAY.

NO ONE KNEW THAT TOM HAD MORE THAN ONE REASON FOR REACHING NANGA-JEVI.

BUT EAGLE SECTION'S FIRST REAL TEST WAS NOT LONG IN COMING.

AHEAD IS CHUKURU VALLEY – A LIKELY PLACE FOR A JAP CAMP.

PERHAPS WE SHOULD GO ROUND IT.

BUT A DETOUR HAD ITS SNAGS.

IT TAKES THREE, FOUR DAYS TO GO ROUND.

WE CAN'T AFFORD THE TIME. IF THE JAPS ARE THERE WE'LL JUST HAVE TO TAKE OUR CHANCES.

BUT TOM AND GANJU WENT AHEAD TO SCOUT FIRST. ACKNOWLEDGED AS THE TWO BEST JUNGLE FIGHTERS, MOVING WITH SPEED, SILENCE AND THE GRACE OF BIG CATS, THEY QUICKLY MELTED INTO THE JUNGLE.

FOR SMOKING ON GUARD, THEY DESERVE TO BE TAUGHT A LESSON, BUT FIRST THINGS FIRST.

STUPID JAPS. MAYBE LATER WE WILL MAKE THEM PAY THE PRICE.

THEIR MINDS WERE CLICKING AS ONE.

THEY REACHED A POSITION OVERLOOKING THE VALLEY AS DAYLIGHT BEGAN TO FADE.

THEY SEEM VERY SURE OF THEMSELVES. WHAT DO YOU THINK, GANJU?

THEY PROBABLY DON'T EXPECT TO FIND THE BRITISH SO CLOSE. THERE LOOKS MAYBE TWO TO THREE HUNDRED OF THEM. MAYBE MORE BEHIND THE HILL.

WHEN THEY MOVED ON, A SECOND CAMP CAME INTO VIEW.

YOU WERE RIGHT. COME ON, LET'S GET BACK.

BUT ON THEIR RETURN, A LOUD JAP VOICE BOOMED OUT.

SERGEANT CATCH SOLDIER WHO SMOKE.

HE WOULDN'T SHOUT LIKE THAT IF HE KNEW WE WERE AROUND.

AS THE SERGEANT AND HIS ESCORT PREPARED TO MOVE ON, LEAVING THE TWO
DISGRUNTLED GUARDS, TOM AND GANJU EXCHANGED GLANCES. THEY HAD DEVELOPED
SUCH A STRONG UNDERSTANDING THAT OFTEN WORDS WERE NOT NECESSARY.

PAH,
SERGEANT SUKATO
IS A BULLYING
PIG.

THE JAPS DIED WITHOUT KNOWING WHO HAD ATTACKED THEM.

UGH!

SWEET
DREAMS, NIP.

A NEARBY SWAMP CLAIMED THE DEAD BODIES AND ALL TRACES OF THE STRUGGLE WERE REMOVED.

IF THESE TWO ARE MISSED BEFORE MORNING, IT'LL LOOK LIKE THEY HAVE DESERTED AFTER THEIR CLASH WITH THE SERGEANT.

GANJU GRINNED... BUT THEN HE CAUGHT SIGHT OF THE TALISMAN AROUND TOM'S NECK. HE REACHED FOR HIS KUKRI, REMEMBERING THE TREACHERY OF HARRINGTON AND TAKITO. FOR IT WAS THE TALISMAN THEY HAD TAKEN FROM HIM.

WHERE DID YOU GET THIS?

IT'S PART OF SOMETHING THAT HAPPENED A LONG TIME AGO. SOMETHING WHICH I HAVE TO PUT RIGHT. WE CAN TALK ABOUT IT LATER, BUT NOT NOW.

BECAUSE HE RESPECTED THE YOUNG OFFICER, GANJU SAID NOTHING AND DECIDED RELUCTANTLY TO WAIT.

THEY HAD NO REAL CHOICE AND THEY ALL KNEW IT.

IT'S A RISK WE'VE GOT TO TAKE. YOU WILL LEAD ONE GROUP AND I WILL TAKE THE OTHER... AND THEN STRAIGHT TO NANGA-JEVI. HEY, WHAT'S GOT INTO GANJU?

NANGA-JEVI SOMEHOW HAS A SPECIAL MEANING FOR HIM, I THINK, AND IT'S TIME I TRIED TO SORT IT OUT.

TOM RUSHED AFTER GANJU, DETERMINED TO FIND OUT THE LITTLE GURKHA'S SECRET.

TELL ME ABOUT NANGA-JEVI AND THAT TALIS-MAN.

THE TALISMAN IS MINE. IT WAS STOLEN WHEN I NEARLY DIED AT NANGA-JEVI.

BUT THEIR PRIVATE PROBLEM HAD TO BE SHELVED, AS THE MEN OF EAGLE FORCE MOVED INTO ACTION IN THE MISTY DAWN.

UGH...

THE JAPS WOULD NOT HAVE SLEPT SO SOUNDLY IF THEY HAD KNOWN THEIR SENTRIES WERE BEING SILENCED.

THE BRITISH MOVED LIKE PHANTOMS AND MANY JAPS DIED LONG BEFORE THE ALARM WAS RAISED.

SLEEP TIGHT, NIP.

IN THE PALE LIGHT OF EARLY DAWN THERE WERE MANY GRIM STRUGGLES.

DEATH TO ENGLISH DOGS... AAAAGH!

TOM'S GROUP STRUCK QUICKLY, LEAVING THE JAPS DISORGANISED AND EVENTUALLY PANIC-STRICKEN.

AFTER 'EM, LADS. WE'VE GOT 'EM ON THE RUN.

BUT MAJOR DAWSON HAD NOT FARED SO WELL, FOR AS HE AND HIS MEN MOVED FORWARD THEY WERE SEEN.

ALARM – ALARM! WE ARE ATTACKED!

AAAAGH!

THE FIGHTING WAS BITTER AS A BRAVE YOUNG JAPANESE OFFICER, LIEUTENANT OSAMU TAKITO, RALLIED HIS MEN.

STAND FIRM, SOLDIERS OF NIPPON. DO NOT GIVE WAY.

OSAMU WAS THE SON OF THE TREACHEROUS TAKITO WHO HAD HELPED TOM'S FATHER STEAL THE EMERALDS.

DAWSON'S MEN GRADUALLY DROVE THE JAPS BACK, BUT LIEUTENANT OSAMU TAKITO CONTROLLED THE WITHDRAWAL LIKE A BATTLE-HARDENED VETERAN. AS EACH GROUP OF JAPANESE RACED FOR COVER THEY WERE PROTECTED BY A BLAST OF FIRE FROM A LINE OF THEIR FELLOW-SOLDIERS.

KEEP FIRING! OUR TURN NEXT.

THE YOUNG LIEUTENANT LED THE SURVIVORS DEEP INTO THE JUNGLE UNTIL THEY HAD SHAKEN OFF PURSUIT.

LET THE MEN REST FOR ONE HOUR. IF I AM NOT BACK BY THEN, GO TO THE CAMP AT NANGA-JEVI. I AM GOING TO FIND OUT THE STRENGTH OF THE BRITISH.

ONE HOUR, EXCELLENCY.

IT SEEMED FATE WAS UNFOLDING A DRAMA WITH NANGA-JEVI AS THE STAGE.

USING ALL THE SKILLS OF A NATURAL HUNTER, OSAMU REACHED A SPOT WHERE HE COULD OBSERVE THE BRITISH FORCE.

THERE ARE MORE OF THEM THAN I THOUGHT.

TOM DIDN'T HESITATE. AS THE TIGER POUNCED HE SQUEEZED THE TRIGGER OF HIS STEN GUN.

GOT YOU, YOU BRUTE!

TOM HAD SAVED HIS ENEMY'S LIFE.

STARTLED, OSAMU SWUNG ROUND AS THE TIGER CRASHED AT HIS FEET. TOM'S AIM HAD BEEN DEADLY.

FOR A MOMENT THE JAP HAD THE DROP ON TOM, BUT HE HELD HIS FIRE. HE COULD NOT UNDERSTAND WHY THE ENGLISHMAN HAD SHOT THE TIGER TO SAVE HIM, BUT HE WAS GRATEFUL.

TOM WAS VULNERABLE BUT THE JAP WAITED UNTIL HE HAD REGAINED HIS FEET, THEN THEY FACED EACH OTHER, GUNS LEVELLED, FINGERS ON THE TRIGGERS.

HE COULD HAVE SHOT ME BUT HE KILLED THE TIGER INSTEAD.

JUST FOR A SECOND I WAS WIDE OPEN. WHY DIDN'T HE SHOOT ME?

THE AIR WAS ELECTRIC — WHOSE GUN WOULD BE THE FIRST TO SPIT DEATH? BUT AS TOM TENSED, READY TO DIVE CLEAR AS HE FIRED, THE JAP SPOKE IN ENGLISH.

YOU KILL TIGER, NOT ME. I THANK YOU, BUT I WILL NOT BE YOUR PRISONER.

NOR WILL I BE YOURS. IT'S STALEMATE.

TOM WAS RIGHT AND THEY BOTH REALISED IT FOR NEITHER MAN COULD BRING HIMSELF
TO PULL THE TRIGGER...AND NEITHER WOULD SURRENDER.

SLOWLY THEY BACKED OFF, EACH SUSPICIOUS OF THE OTHER, UNTIL THE JUNGLE
SWALLOWED THEM UP.

TOM WOULD HAVE BEEN AMAZED IF HE HAD KNOWN WHO HIS ENEMY WAS – AS WOULD
OSAMU. BUT FATE HAD DESTINED THAT THE TWO SONS OF THE ROBBERS OF THE NANGA-
JEVI EMERALDS WOULD MEET AGAIN.

OSAMU HAD BEEN TAUGHT THAT ALL ENGLISHMEN WERE
WITHOUT HONOUR, BUT NOW THE SEEDS OF DOUBT WERE SOWN.

THE YOUNG TAKITO FOUND HIS MEN RESTED AND READY TO MOVE. THE BASE CAMP OF NANGA-JEVI HAD TO BE WARNED AND HE HAD NO RADIO.

WE MUST REACH NANGA-JEVI AS QUICKLY AS POSSIBLE. THEY MUST BE WARNED OF THE ENEMY ADVANCE.

BY FORCED MARCHING THEY REACHED THE BASE CAMP THREE DAYS LATER WHERE A SURPRISE WAS IN STORE FOR OSAMU.

OSAMU, IT IS GOOD TO SEE YOU ARE SAFE.

YOU MUST COME AND DRINK SAKI WITH US WHEN YOU ARE RESTED.

I HARDLY KNOW THESE MEN. WHY DO THEY GREET ME IN THIS WAY?

IN THE OFFICERS' QUARTERS, OSAMU QUICKLY FOUND HE WAS THE CENTRE OF ATTRACTION.

I AM DREAMING! THEY DO NOT DRINK TO ME FOR BRINGING BACK SURVIVORS. I AM NOT A HERO.

LATER, TAKO, HIS FRIEND AND FELLOW OFFICER, EXPLAINED.

YOU HEARD OUR COMMANDANT WAS KILLED BY LOCAL TRIBESMEN? WELL, HIS SUCCESSOR ARRIVES TOMORROW.

SO WHAT HAS THIS TO DO WITH ME?

THE ANSWER MADE HIM ANGRY.

BECAUSE THEY WANT YOU TO SPEAK WELL OF THEM WHEN THE NEW COMMANDANT ARRIVES... OUR NEW C.O. IS YOUR FATHER, COLONEL TAKITO.

WHAT! MY FATHER COMING HERE? THEN I WILL ASK FOR A TRANSFER. I WILL NOT SERVE UNDER HIM IF I CAN HELP IT.

OSAMU KNEW THAT HIS FATHER WAS HATED AND FEARED. HE HAD JOINED THE ARMY BEFORE THE WAR AND RISEN SWIFTLY, THANKS TO HIS RUTHLESS BRUTALITY.

BUT WHEN HE ARRIVED THE FOLLOWING DAY, COLONEL TAKITO WAS IN A JOVIAL MOOD. AT LAST, AFTER PULLING MANY STRINGS, HE HAD ACHIEVED THE POSTING HE CRAVED FOR. THE EMERALDS OF NANGA-JEVI WOULD SOON BE IN HIS HANDS, AND SO FAR THE CURSE HAD NOT TROUBLED HIM.

WELCOME TO NANGA-JEVI, EX-CELLENCY. THE MEN ARE READY FOR YOUR IN-SPECTION.

DISMISS, THEM, MAJOR, AND ISSUE A RATION OF SAKI TO EACH MAN.

THIS IS NOT LIKE MY FATHER. THEY WILL SOON DISCOVER WHAT HE IS REALLY LIKE.

AS THE COLONEL TURNED AWAY HE CAUGHT SIGHT OF HIS SON. THERE WAS NO LOVE LOST BETWEEN THEM. HE HAD HEARD OF OSAMU'S COURAGE AND SKILL, AND HE WAS JEALOUS.

SO! THE GREAT HERO, EH? WHO HAVE YOU FOUGHT AGAINST — THE BRITISH? PAH, THEY ARE LIKE WOMEN!

AS YOU SAY, EXCELLENCY.

OSAMU WOULD NOT BE DRAWN TO ANGER. HE HAD ACCEPTED HIS FATHER'S INSULTS, BUT THERE WAS HATRED IN HIS HEART.

OSAMU HAD NEVER DEFIED HIS FATHER... TO DO SO WOULD DISGRACE THE FAMILY NAME AND CAUSE HIS FATHER TO LOSE FACE. THE COLONEL KNEW THIS AND HIS TAUNTS BIT DEEPER.

THEY HAD GUESSED HIS MOOD CORRECTLY. IT WAS WISER TO RIDICULE THE SON THAN INCUR THE DISPLEASURE OF THE FATHER.

URGENT NEWS OF THE ADVANCE OF THE BRITISH BROUGHT OSAMU WELCOME RELIEF.

MEANWHILE THE MEN OF EAGLE SECTION WERE MOVING NEARER.

WHY HAVEN'T THEY ATTACKED US YET? THEY MUST KNOW WE'RE HERE.

IT'S AN OLD HUNTING TRICK TO LET YOUR VICTIMS GROW CONFIDENT. THEN THE KILL COMES WHEN YOU'RE NOT EX-PECTING IT. BUT YOU CAN BE SURE THEY KNOW WE ARE HERE.

AS USUAL, GANJU WAS RIGHT. SLANT EYES WATCHED THEIR PROGRESS FROM WELL-CONCEALED OBSERVATION POSTS.

ENEMY PASSING NINE-O-THREE.

GOOD. THEY ARE WALKING INTO MY TRAP. IT IS TIME FOR YOU TO LEAVE, OSAMU.

THE COLONEL HAD A SUDDEN URGE TO TELL HIS SON THE SECRET HE HAD KEPT FOR OVER THIRTEEN YEARS.

WHEN I HAVE DISPOSED OF THESE BRITISH, I SHALL AT LAST RETRIEVE MY EMERALDS.

WHAT EMERALDS?

CONFIDENT OF SUCCESS, TAKITO TOLD OF HIS THEFT. BUT –

THIS IS A BAD THING. IT IS NOT WISE...

GET OUT, DOLT. BREATHE ONE WORD TO ANY MAN, AND I WILL HAVE YOUR HEAD!

OSAMU HAD NO TIME TO DWELL ON HIS FATHER'S CRIMES. HE AND HIS MEN TOOK UP THEIR POSITIONS AS THE BRITISH SOLDIERS APPROACHED...

AAGH!

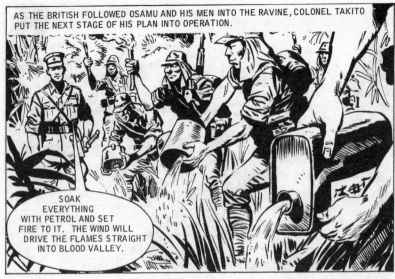

WITHIN MINUTES THE SURVIVORS OF EAGLE SECTION WERE ASSEMBLED AND THE NATIVES LED THEM TO A ROCK FACE.

THIS IS NO WAY OUT. WE'LL NEVER CLIMB UP THERE.

BUT CLIMBING WASN'T NECESSARY.

THIS OPENING LEADS TO THE CENTRE OF MOUNTAIN.

LEAD ON. I'LL BRING UP THE REAR.

PROGRESS WAS SLOW AND TOM MADE THE SAFETY OF THE NARROW ROCK CLEFT WITH ONLY SECONDS TO SPARE.

A FEW MORE SECONDS AND I'D HAVE HAD IT.

THE CHIEF OF THE NEPALTA TRIBE WAS WAITING FOR THEM. CHIEF KABOTO HAD NO LOVE FOR THE JAPANESE CONQUERORS OF HIS COUNTRY.

THANK YOU, YOU SAVED OUR LIVES.

JAPANESE KILL MANY OF MY PEOPLE, MAKE OTHERS WORK, BUILD ROADS. WHEN YOU AND MEN RESTED I SHOW YOU HOW TO THANK ME FOR SAVING LIVES.

AFTER A SHORT REST THEY WERE GUIDED UP THROUGH THE CENTRE OF THE MOUNTAIN, ALL THE TIME CLIMBING HIGHER AND HIGHER. THOUGH HE DID NOT KNOW IT YET, TOM SCOTT HAD FINALLY REACHED NANGA-JEVI, BUT NOT BY THE ROUTE HE HAD INTENDED.

PHEW, TALK ABOUT OUT OF THE FRYING PAN AND INTO THE FIRE.

WHEN THE SMOKE CLEARED IT WAS ALL OVER. THE LEDGE WAS A SCENE OF DEATH AND DEVASTATION.

FOR THE FIRST TIME SINCE TOM HAD REVEALED HIS TRUE IDENTITY, GANJU'S MANNER WAS WARM AND FRIENDLY.

AS THE LAST OF HIS MEN FILTERED OUT FROM THE CAVERN, TOM GAVE ORDERS FOR THE ATTACK ON THE JAP BASE CAMP OF NANGA-JEVI, USING THE JAPS' OWN FIELD GUN.

THE FIGHTING WAS HARD AND BITTER — NO QUARTER ASKED OR GIVEN.

BUT THE ODDS WERE TOO GREAT. AS ONE JAP FELL IT SEEMED AS IF THERE WAS ANOTHER TO TAKE HIS PLACE.

TOM WISHED TO STAY — HE STILL HAD TO PUT RIGHT HIS FATHER'S WRONG, BUT PERSONAL PROBLEMS HAD NO PLACE HERE. HIS FIRST CONCERN WAS THE SAFETY OF HIS MEN.

WHEN IT SEEMED THAT THE YELLOW TIDE WOULD ENGULF THEM, A FUSILLADE OF SHOTS TORE INTO THE JAPANESE ATTACKERS.   HELP HAD ARRIVED.

THE MEN OF SNOWDROP FORCE TURNED THE TABLES, AND THE JAPS BEGAN TO CRUMBLE.

CONCERNED ONLY FOR HIS OWN SKIN TAKITO TURNED AND FLED, DESERTING HIS MEN LIKE THE RAT HE WAS – BUT HE WAS SEEN.

MEANWHILE, THE JAPS, BATTERED INTO SUBMISSION AND LEADERLESS, WERE BEING ROUNDED UP. INSTINCTIVELY, AS IF DRIVEN BY SOME STRANGE POWER, TOM RACED AFTER GANJU.

BUT GANJU KNEW WHAT HE WAS DOING AS HE FOLLOWED TAKITO'S TRAIL. AT LENGTH HE EMERGED INTO THE CLEARING BY MONKEY ROCK TO FIND TAKITO RETRIEVING THE STOLEN TREASURE.

AS TAKITO GLOATED OVER THE PRICELESS EMERALDS, GANJU CALLED TO HIM IN A GRIM VOICE FULL OF MENACE.

TAKITO, REMEMBER ME?

DON'T SHOOT! LOOK, YOU CAN HAVE HALF OF THESE. YOU'LL BE RICH.

GANJU HAD NO INTENTION OF SHOOTING. HIS PERSONAL HONOUR COULD BE SATISFIED ONLY BY THE TRADITIONAL KUKRI KNIFE.

DEATH BY A BULLET IS TOO EASY. YOU WILL DIE SLOWLY...

NO, NO — TAKE ALL THE JEWELS!

BUT AS HE SPOKE, THE TREACHEROUS TAKITO DIVED FOR HIS PISTOL, PUMPING THE TRIGGER AS HE ROLLED OVER.

THE JAP'S MAGAZINE WAS SOON EMPTY. AND GANJU, HIT IN THE SHOULDER, STILL CAME ON. AT THAT MOMENT TOM SCOTT BURST THROUGH THE TREES —

BUT BEFORE GANJU COULD TAKE HIS REVENGE, ANOTHER FIGURE EMERGED FROM THE TREES.

EVERY EYE WAS TURNED ON OSAMU, THE SOLE SURVIVING JAP WHO HAD SOMEHOW ESCAPED FROM THE FURNACE... ESCAPED WHEN ANYONE LESS SKILLED IN CLIMBING WOULD HAVE BURNED TO DEATH.

AS OSAMU MOVED FORWARD TOWARDS TOM AND GANJU, TAKITO SAW HIS CHANCES OF SALVATION SLIPPING AWAY.

THE KNOWLEDGE THAT TAKITO WAS THE YOUNG JAP LIEUTENANT'S FATHER SET TOM WONDERING.

BUT GANJU'S HOT ANGER COOLED AS TOM SPOKE.

KILL HIM IN COLD BLOOD, AND YOU'LL REGRET IT.

YES, YOU ARE RIGHT. WE'LL TAKE HIM TO BE PUNISHED FOR WHAT HE'S DONE.

BUT TAKITO WOULD NEVER BE TRIED FOR HIS CRIMES. A SPEAR STREAKED THROUGH THE AIR...

AAAGH!

OLD KABOTO, CHIEF OF THE NEPALTA, HAD SETTLED THE ACCOUNT. THE CURSE OF NANGA-JEVI HAD CLAIMED ITS SECOND VICTIM.

HE WAS DEVIL! HE WAS MAN WHO HURT GURU AND STEAL PRECIOUS STONES FROM OUR GOD.

SO, WITH THE EXHAUSTED JAP BETWEEN THEM, TOM AND GANJU WERE GUIDED BY THE NEPALTA TO THE OLD GURU.

COME CLOSER, MY SONS. NO CURSE WILL HARM YOU NOW.

THEY RETURNED THE JEWELS BACK INTO THE OLD MAN'S KEEPING.

MANY BLESSINGS UPON YOU, MY FRIENDS. FROM THIS DAY THE HOUSES OF HARRINGTON AND TAKITO WILL BE UNITED AND MUCH RESPECTED. GO IN PEACE.

LATER, ARRANGEMENTS WERE MADE FOR OSAMU TO BE MOVED TO PRISON HOSPITAL, WHERE HE STAYED UNTIL THE END OF THE WAR — FIRST AS A PATIENT, LATER AS A TRUSTED HELPER.

GOODBYE, OSAMU. WHEN ALL THIS IS OVER WE SHALL MEET AGAIN.

GOODBYE.

FAREWELL. I HOPE WE SHALL ALL BE REAL FRIENDS ONE DAY.

AND AT LAST NANGA-JEVI WAS IN BRITISH HANDS. THERE WOULD BE NO MORE RETREATING, AND TOM AND GANJU WERE TWO WHO WOULD BE ALWAYS WHERE THE FIGHTING WAS FIERCEST.

THE COVERS

No. 668

Commando

WAR STORIES IN PICTURES

6p

FIGHT TO THE FINISH

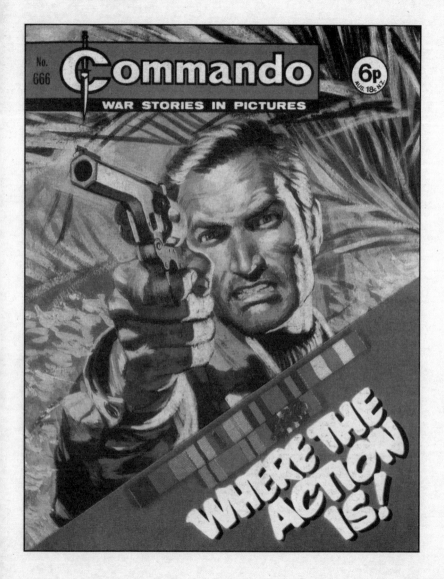